Anna Seward

Louisa

A poetical novel, in four epistles. Fourth Edition

Anna Seward

Louisa
A poetical novel, in four epistles. Fourth Edition

ISBN/EAN: 9783337045364

Printed in Europe, USA, Canada, Australia, Japan

Cover: Foto ©Andreas Hilbeck / pixelio.de

More available books at **www.hansebooks.com**

L O U I S A,

A

P O E T I C A L   N O V E L,

I N

F O U R   E P I S T L E S.

B Y   M I S S   S E W A R D.

T H E   F O U R T H   E D I T I O N.

L I C H F I E L D:

Printed and Sold by J. Jackson, and G. Robinson,
in Pater-Noster-Row, London,
MDCCLXXXIV.

THE ensuing epistolary poems contain a description rather of passions than of incidents. They resulted from an idea of it being possible to unite the impassion'd fondness of POPE's ELOISA, with the chaster tenderness of PRIOR's EMMA; avoiding the voluptuousness of the first, and the too conceding softness of the second. It is hoped the Reader will distinguish between the apprehended possibility of exhibiting in verse a more faultless female Character than the ELOISA of POPE, or the EMMA of PRIOR, and the rash and vain design of equalling, much less of surpassing the transcendent poetic excellence of either of those Compositions.

THE LOUISA of the following pages has all that enthusiasm which springs from an heart warmly affectionate, joined to a glowing and picturesque imagination. Her sensibilities, heightened, and refined in the bosom of Retirement, know no bounds, except those which the dignity of conscious Worth, and a strong sense of Religion prescribe. It is feared the modern young Ladies will have little sympathy with her, since she is unfashionably enthusiastic, and unfashionably tender.

AN ingenious Friend, after reading the first epistle, remarked, that LOUISA might have described with more interesting particularity her Lover's declaration of his passion, and the manner in which she received that declaration; but the Author thought the present method of conveying that circumstance to the mind of the Reader more poetic. POPE's ELOISA is minute in her description of the awful Scenery, formed by the rocks, the streams, and mountains of Paraclete, but by no means minute concerning the amorous eclaircissement between herself and Abelard. LOUISA discriminates her Lover's *early* attentions to her, tho' she leaves the manner of his declaring their source very much to the Imagination.

B

Her

P R E F A C E.

Her application of the beautiful fcenic objects, by which fhe was at that interval furrounded, to her own, and to her Lover's fituation ; and the paffing fuddenly to their prefent altered appearance, contrafts the charms, and bloom of the firft, with the chill drearinefs of the fecond. There it was that the Author had in view that ftriking letter in the 3d Vol. of the Nouvelle-Heloife, which defcribes St. Preaux accompanying Mrs. Wolmar to the rocks of Meillerie, then covered with the richnefs of Summer-luxuriance ; and painting to her the fituation of that very Scene, when he had vifited it alone, amidft the horrors of Winter, and found thofe horrors congenial to the temper of his Soul.

This Poem has little chance to be popular. A feeling Heart, and a fondnefs for Verfe muft *unite* to render it interefting. A feeling Heart without a glowing Imagination will be tired of the Landfcape-painting, fomewhat luxuriantly interfperfed. An Imagination that glows, while the Heart is frozen, has a propenfity to fancy every thing profaic which is not imagery, and will probably yawn over the reafon-ing of thefe Lovers, and ficken over their tendernefs.

If, however, this little Work has the honor to intereft and pleafe the Few, in whom the kind and fweet affections are blended with poetic tafte, the end for which it is publifhed will be obtained.

Except fome flight alterations, which have been made fince the two firft Editions, the hundred and fifty fix lines, with which the poem opens, were written when the Author was only nineteen. They had been miflaid during a long interval. It is fixteen months fince they were accidentally recovered. Some few Friends, to whom the Frag-ment was fhewn, thought it worth being extended into a regular Work. The firft, and third of thefe epiftles are defigned to be def-criptive, and fentimental ; the fecond, and laft, dramatic.

L O U I S A

E M M A,

HER FRIEND IN THE EAST-INDIES.

OCTOBER 21, 1779.

THEE, EMMA, four flow-circling years have feen
 Prefs, with thy penfive foot, Savannas green;
Seen thee, with fond Affection's moiften'd gaze,
And the low-warbled fong of former days,
Wind round the fhadowy Rock, and fhelving Glade,
Where broad Bananas ftretch their grateful fhade;
Bend o'er the Weft thy longing eyes, and chide
The tardy Breeze that fans th' unfreighted Tide.

Now, as with filial care thy light ftep roves,
Thro' India's palmy plains, and fpicy groves,

To blefs thee, exil'd thus in Youth's gay prime,
May fprightly Health refift the torrid clime,
Temper the fickly blaft, the fever'd ray,
And Peace, and Pleafure, lead the fhining Day!
Yet, when thou know'ft for me, that Sorrow fhrouds
Hope's cryftal mirror with impervious clouds,
The fighs, and tears, that tendereft pity fpeak,
Shall fwell thy breaft, and chill thy glowing cheek;
Since one have been our pleafures, one our cares,
From the firft dawn of thofe delicious years,
What time, infpir'd by joy's enlivening powers,
We chas'd the gilded Infect thro' the bowers;
And oh! I fondly tell my anxious heart,
The deareft truth experience can impart,
That yet, to quench this fympathy of foul,
Time, and the world of waters, vainly roll.

O'er this deep Glen, departing Autumn throws,
With kind reverted glance, a fhort repofe,
E'er yet fhe leaves her ENGLAND's fading fcene,
Where fickly yellow ftains the vivid green,

And

And many an icy morn, and ftormy gale
Embrown the pathway of the winding vale.

Now, while I feek the bofom of the Glade,
And the thin fhelter of th' impoverifh'd Shade,
Unequal fteps, and rifing fighs, difclofe
The thorny preffure of tyrannic woes;
And where th' incumbent Rock, with awful face,
Bends o'er the fountain, gurgling from its bafe,
And marks the limit of the filent Dell,
Sadly I fit my bofom'd griefs to tell;
Invoke thy Spirit, thofe fond griefs to footh,
And bid, alas! their furging tide be fmooth.

It will not be ;—fince here, with yearning thought,
By weak, involuntary impulfe brought,
Where Love and Memory bear refiftlefs fway,
And all the weaknefs of the Soul betray!

O ye known objects!—how ye ftrike my heart!
And vain regrets, with keener force, impart!

Slow

Slow, thro' the faded grove, paft Pleafures glide,
Or fadly linger by the fountain's fide.

Dear, awful witnefs of a broken vow,
Steep Rock, how fternly frowns thy rugged brow!
But, if the frequent blaft fhall bend thy pines,
Clear at thy foot the cryftal water fhines!
Tho' drizzling Clouds the mifty Mountains veil,
Yet the mild Sun-beam gilds the narrow Dale!
Tho' vernal flow'rs this bank no more adorn,
Nor Summer's wild-rofe blufhes on its thorn,
Yet fhelter'd, moffy, dry, and warm, it draws
The heedlefs roving ftep to quiet paufe.

Thus the pale Year, tho' Nature's edicts urge
Her ftep to Winter's defolating verge,
Sedately paffes to the drear domain,
And breathes, e'en yet, foft comforts o'er the plain;
But oh! for me, in Youth's luxuriant glow,
Hope's lovely florets wither as they blow!

No

No grief my bofom at our parting knew,
But that of bidding thee a long adieu;
And the fweet tears, that fuch foft forrows bring,
Fall, as light rain-drops in the funny Spring;
For youthful Hope, fubduing tender Fears,
Bounds o'er the gulf of interpofing Years;
While, thro' their courfe, her airy hands avert
Misfortune's arrow from the Wanderer's heart.

Soon then did Cheerfulnefs the morn illume,
And Peace defcend with Evening's grateful gloom;
They faw my breaft in that clear fpirit gay,
Which fpeeds the focial hour fo faft away.

Now Expectation's fervour rofe, to hail
The youthful Mafter of this quiet Vale,
My blooming Brother—from Oxonia's towers,
Who fought, with tender hafte, his native bowers.

'Twas Noon, and ripen'd Summer's fervid ray
From cloudlefs Ether fhed oppreffive day.

As

As on this fhady bank I fat reclin'd,
My voice, that floated on the waving wind,
Taught the foft echos of the neighboring plains
Milton's fweet lays, in Handel's matchlefs ftrains.
Prefaging notes my lips unconfcious try,
And murmur—" * Hide me from Day's garifh eye !
Ah ! bleft, had Death beneath his fable fhrine
Hid me from all the woes that fince were mine !

Beneath my trembling fingers lightly rung
The Lute's fweet chords, refponfive while I fung.
Faint in the yellow broom the Oxen lay,
And the mute Birds fat languid on the fpray ;
And nought was heard, around the noon-tide bower,
Save, that the mountain Bee, from flower to flower,
Seem'd to prolong, with her affiduous wing,
The foft vibration of the tuneful ftring ;
While the fierce Skies flam'd on the fhrinking Rills,
And fultry Silence brooded o'er the Hills !

As on my lip the lingering cadence play'd,
My Brother gaily bounded down the glade,

* An enchanting Song of Handel's, from Milton's Il Penferofo.

And,

And, while my looks the fire of gladnefs dart,
With ardor prefs'd me to his throbbing heart;
Then to a graceful Stranger turn'd, whofe feet,
With fteps lefs fwift, my coyer welcome meet.
O'er his fine form, and o'er his glowing face,
Youth's ripen'd bloom had fhed its richeft grace;
Tall as the Pine, amidft inferior Trees,
With all the bending Ozier's pliant eafe.
O'er his fair brow, the fairer for their fhade,
Locks of the warmeft brown luxuriant play'd.
Blufhing he bows!—and gentle awe fupplies
Each flattering meaning to his downcaft eyes;
Sweet, ferious, tender, thofe blue eyes impart
A thoufand dear fenfations to the heart;
Mild as the Evening Star whofe fhining ray
Soft in th' unruffled Water feems to play;
And when he fpeaks—not Mufic's thrilling pow'r,
No, not the vocal Miftrefs of the bow'r,
When flow fhe warbles from the bloffom'd fpray,
In liquid blandifhment, her evening lay,
Such foft infinuating fweetnefs knows,
As from that voice in melting accent flows!

Yet

Yet why, fond Memory ! why, in tints fo warm,
Paint'ft thou each beauty of that faultlefs Form?
His fpecious virtues furely might impart
Excufe more juft for this devoted heart.
Oh ! how each noble paffion's feeming trace,
Threw tranfient glories o'er his youthful face !
How rofe, with fudden impulfe, fwift, and ftrong,
For ev'ry fecret fraud, and open wrong
Th' Oppreffor acts, the Helplefs feel, or fear,
Difdain's quick throb, and Pity's melting tear !
So well its part each ductile feature play'd,
Of worth, fuch firm, tho' filent promife made,
That to have doubted its well painted truth,
Had been to want the primal grace of youth
Credulity, that fcorns, with gen'rous heat,
Alike to practice, or fufpect deceit.

Ceafe, vain Regrets, excurfive Fancy ceafe !
Ye only wound afrefh my bleeding peace,
And keep from gentle E M M A's anxious ear
Th' event fhe longs, yet kindly dreads, to hear ;

But

But ah ! nor fingular, nor ftrange the tale,
My Sifter-Sufferers mourn in every vale ;
For gold, and dazzling ftate, inceffant prove,
In Man's hard heart, the Murderers of Love.

While many a Sun in Summer-glory rofe,
EUGENIO's lip no fofter accent knows
Than Friendfhip dictates—but diforder'd praife,
Scarce half exprefs'd ; the mufing ardent gaze ;
The varying cheek ; the frequent fmother'd figh,
Reveal the latent meaning of his eye ;
Plain, and yet plainer ev'ry hour, declare
The fhining fecrecies, that languifh there.

Thefe are the days that fly on Rapture's wing,
Empurpling ev'ry flower that decks the Spring ;
For when delicious Hope, with whifper bland,
Wakes the dear magic of her potent wand,
More vivid colours paint the rifing Morn,
And clearer cryftal gems the filver thorn ;
On more luxuriant fhade the Noon-beam plays,
And richer gold the Evening-Sun arrays ;

Stars

Stars feem to glitter with enamour'd fire,
And fhadowy Hills in ftatelier grace afpire ;
More fubtle fweetnefs fcents the paffing gales,
And fofter beauty decks the moon-light Vales ;
All Nature fmiles ! nor e'en the jocund Day,
When feftal rofes ftrew the bridal way,
Darts thro' the Virgin breaft fuch keen delight,
As when foft Fears with gay Belief unite ;
As Hope, fweet, warm, feducing Hope infpires,
Which fomewhat queftions, what it moft defires ;
Reads latent meaning in a Lover's eye,
Thrills at his glance, and trembles at his figh ;
As o'er the Frame diforder'd tranfport pours,
When only lefs than Certainty is ours.

At length, that rofy Certainty appears,
With faithlefs promifes of golden years.
Here, by this fountain fide, EUGENIO ftrove
To trace the tender progrefs of his love ;
'Twas on the Evening of a fplendid Day ;—
Calm on the gilded grafs the fountain lay !

But

But oh! when doubt, in that dear moment, fled,
A calm more funny o'er my bofom fpread!

As the gay Lark his laſt clear carol fung,
And on a flanting Sun-beam warbling hung,
With fweeter mufic trill'd the vefper lay,
Than when he foar'd amid the blaze of Day;
But yet a thoufand times more fweet the found,
In which my Soul its deareſt blefling found!

Slow on the Sun had ſtol'n the failing Cloud,
And drawn o'er his gay fires the purple ſhroud,
Then roll'd away!—till, by no ſhade repreft,
Afar the fetting Orb emblaz'd the Weſt;
Lighted with arrowy beams the Ocean caves,
And funk with fplendor in the illumin'd waves!

Thus oft would Modeſty her bluſh employ,
Coyly to veil the radiance of my joy;
But from thefe eyes the fun-bright gladnefs beam'd,
And all the triumph of my bofom ſtream'd!

'Twas

'Twas here,—e'en here!—where now I fit reclined,
And Winter's fighs found hollow in the Wind;
Loud, and more loud the blaft of Evening raves,
And ftrips the Oaks of their laft, lingering leaves;
The eddying foliage in the tempeft flies,
And fills with dufkier gloom the thickning Skies.
Red finks the Sun, behind the howling Hill,
And rufhes, with hoarfe ftream, the mountain Rill,
And now, with ruffling billow, cold, and pale,
Runs, fwoln, and dafhing, down the lonely Vale;
While, to thefe tear-full eyes, Grief's faded form,
Sits on the Cloud, and fighs amid the Storm!

Yet, dreary Vale! detain thy penfive Gueft,
Tho' drizzling fleet beats cold upon her breaft!
To this fad Soul more welcome are thy glooms,
Than Spring's green bowers, or Summer's gaudy blooms;
Nor afks an Heart, that only breathes to figh,
A warmer manfion, or a kinder Sky!

And ftill that deftin'd Heart, fo fond to mourn,
And dwell on fcenes, which never can return,

Shrinks,

Shrinks, e'en as guilty bofoms fhrink from fhame,
To join with *Perfidy* EUGENIO's name;
Feels its foft ftreams in ev'ry pulfe recede
From the pain'd mention of one barborous deed,
That kills my hopes, like Eurus' fierce career
On the bright foliage of the early year;
Which turns, while premature its buds difclofe,
To livid yellownefs the damafk Rofe.

Thou fee'ft, my EMMA with what fond delay
Th' uuwilling Spirit loiters on her way;
Clings to paft fcenes that wore gay Summer's form;
Clings to the wildnefs of the wintry Storm,
To ftop the fad narration, e'er it throw,
Dark on my fate, the long, long night of Woe.

Yet, O my Soul! refume it, e'er the power
Of wafting Sicknefs brings the fever'd Hour,
That ftops th' ill-guided pen in the weak hand,
And fhakes from Life's dim glafs the ebbing fand!

Thou,

Thou, E M M A, wilt not blame my eafy youth,
That foon this Heart declar'd its tendereft truth.
Ah ! could I dream he feign'd, whofe glances warm
With ceafelefs ardor wander'd o'er my form ?
And as gay fmiles, and youthful graces fair,
Shone in my eyes, and harmoniz'd my air,
Not one unheeded pafs'd his eager gaze,
His fervent, yet difcriminating praife ;
Tho' oft he fwore, amid the fond furvey,
The Mind they grac'd was lovelier far than they ;
Protefted oft, that Mind was form'd to fhare
Each high-foul'd purpofe, and each virtuous care ;
Catch ev'ry new idea, as it rofe,
Partake his joys, and melt with all his woes ;
Falfe could I think that vow, whofe ftarting tear
Sprung, the warm witnefs of a faith fincere ?

Now dawn'd th' appointed, but unwelcome Day,
That bore my deareft Brother far away,
Where foreign Climes might ftore his ripening Youth,
With Obfervation, Science, Tafte, and Truth.

The

The fame fad Day my lov'd EUGENIO figh'd
Adieus impaffion'd to his promis'd Bride;
Yet often urg'd, infpiring faithlefs cafe,
That between *us* Fate fpread no cruel *Seas*;
Alas! in his chang'd Heart my eyes explore,
Of Falfehood's waves,—a Sea,—without a Shore!

Where Thames expands with Freedom's wealthy pride,
Attractive Commerce calls him to her Tide;
As with firm ftep fhe runs along the Strand,
And points to the tall Ship, the diftant Land.
His rifing interefts on the call attend,
For with a Father's profperous fate they blend.
Thus, with thefe interefts, Duty's filial power
Unites to tear him from LOUISA's bower;
But parting Sorrows yield them to the force
Of ftrong Neceffity's refiftlefs courfe,
By generous Confidence when lull'd to reft,
That broods, on dove-like pinion, o'er the breaft;
While, from kind letters, rays of joy pervade
The gloomy moments of the love-fick Maid;

D

And

And oh! how warm, who bright thofe letters glow'd,
What ardent Love, in melting language flow'd,
My deareft EMMA, thou wilt ne'er explore;
The brilliant Talifmans are mine no more!
Pride, Virgin-Pride, pronounc'd the ftern beheft,
And tore the faithlefs Scriptures from my breaft!

Thro' four fweet months, to my delighted eyes
Thefe precious tablets of my blifs arife!
At length, dread Silence,—torturing Doubt, and Fear,
Prompt the pang'd figh—but check the fofter tear;
Thro' the lone Day, and lonelier Night, impart
" The Hope deferr'd, that maketh fick the Heart."
Wifh'd Morning comes!—and Hour fucceeds to Hour!
But ftill, Sufpenfe, and Terror o'er me lower;
Chace each conjecture kind, with fierce controul,
And fend their cruel ice-bolt thro' my foul.

Three wretched weeks my throbbing bofom bears
The wounding conflict of its various fears.
While Rumour's voice inflames my grief, and pride,
And gives EUGENIO to a wealthier Bride.

My

My trembling hands, the sick suspense to ease,
From Day to Day the public records seize;
While glances, rapid as the meteor's ray,
Eager amidst the crouded columns stray;
Snatch at sad Certainty from busy Fame,
Yet dread to meet my dear E u g e n i o's Name.

Now glooms on the stain'd page the barborous Truth,
And blights each blooming promise of my youth!
E u g e n i o *married!*—Anguish, and Despair,
In ev'ry pompous killing letter glare!
Thy Love, a Sacrifice to glut thy Pride!—
Ah! what avail the riches of thy Bride!
Can they avail, remorseless as thou art,
To tear the wrong'd L o u i s a from thy heart?

Gold, and ye Gems, that lurk in Eastern Cave,
Or to the Sun your gay resplendence wave,
Can joys sincere, one heart-felt transport live
In ought ye purchase, or in ought ye give?
A Bliss, to rival those thy avarice lost,
Insolvent I n d i a shall but vainly boast!

Was

Was it for *this* my gentle Brother's heart
Bore in our growing loves fo warm a part!
That foft Indulgence deck'd his open brows,
That Smiles fraternal hail'd our mutual vows!
And, as he kindly breath'd the parting figh,
Love's cryftal fluid rufhing to his eye,
Was it for *this* our blooming Hopes he bleft,
Seiz'd our twined hands, and clafp'd them to his breaft?
Ah! did he know his lov'd L o u i s a's fate,
What Energy would nerve his rifing Hate!
Hafte, my L o r e n z o, to thy Sifter's aid!
With thy fwift vengeance be her wrongs repaid!
Ye rifing Winds, his wandering Sails reftore!
Ye refluent Waters, bear him to the Shore!

And thou, vain Bride! enjoy the Meteor-ray,
The fancied fun-beam of thy nuptial Day!
Stern Fury waits, to quench its tranfient light,
In deep, enfanguin'd, everlafting Night!
Bleed, Faithlefs, bleed!—L o u i s a's Wrongs explor'd,
Shall frown relentlefs on her Brother's fword!

—Rafh,

—Rafh, loft Louisa!—could'ft thou bear the ftrife?
Throw on a fatal chance thy Brother's life?
Or ftretch, a victim to thy proud difdain,
Eugenio, pale, and bleeding, on the plain?
Endure that from a bofom, once fo dear,
Convulfive pangs the trembling Life fhould tear?
Oh! fhould'ft thou, certain of the cruel truth,
Behold, in Fancy's eye, the flaughter'd Youth,
Could'ft thou that lov'd, that lovely Form furvey,
And fee it faded to infenfate Clay?
Eternal darknefs on thofe eye-lids hung?
Eternal filence ftiffen on that tongue?
No! wildly, from the bare furmife, I ftart,
And treble fondnefs rufhes thro' my heart;
Live!—live Eugenio!—free from fierce alarms,
Bleft, if thou can'ft, e'en in my Rival's arms!
O! fafe, thro' lengthen'd years, may'ft thou remain
From all the varied forms of deathful Pain!
From injur'd Honor's unrelenting ire,
The blaft of Accident, the Fever's fire!
Soft may thofe dangerous graces melt away,
And gently fink in fcarce perceiv'd decay!

For

For this my breaft its curelefs woes fhall hide,
Nor fting fraternal Love, nor generous Pride.
Yes, dear LORENZO! thou fhalt ftill believe,
Tho' much the thought thy gentle breaft will grieve,
LOUISA, loft to tendernefs, and truth,
In the vain levity of thoughtlefs Youth,
Prov'd to EUGENIO's love a cold Ingrate,
And lightly fplenetic *deferv'd* her fate.

Cruel Rememberance! how fhall I affuage
The yearning pangs of thy inceffant rage?
What balmy comfort can the Heart pervade,
When bitter tears his broken faith upbraid,
Whofe hand, we fondly hop'd, fhould wipe away
Their flowing forrows thro' each future Day?
Since in Reflection's grafp each Bleffing dies,
When the forc'd ftruggling Spirit muft defpife
Him who, encircled with Perfection's zone,
Long in our fight fcarce lefs than Angel fhone.
For if Credulity her warmth impart,
With veils of Light fhe fcreens the felfifh Heart;

But

But barborous Perfidy's fevere extreme,
In fhades eternal, fhrouds each gorgeous beam.

On the arch'd windows thus, that proudly grace
An high majeftic Temple's awful face,
When pours the fetting Sun its darting rays,
An hundred folar Orbs appear to blaze;
But when th' incumbent fhades of lowering Night
Curtain the fource of this illufive light,
Its evanefcent fires no more remain,
But Horrors gather round the darken'd Fane;
The lofty Turrets, defolately grand,
In dreary ftate, and lonely filence ftand;
Thro' the dim Ailes pale Spectres feem to fleet,
And hollow groans the whifpering Walls repeat.

So round EUGENIO's form, that rifes yet,
'Mid Pride's cold frown, and Paffion's warm regret,
Depriv'd of all the luftre it retain'd,
When gay Belief with funny hue remain'd,
Inceffant now the Fiends of avarice glide,
With dark Ambition fcowling at their fide.

Detefted

Detefted impotence of flatter'd charms,
That could not bind my Wanderer to my arms!
Ah! what avail'd your beauties, but to lure
That fleeting Love, ye knew not to fecure!

Like opening flow'rs, that deck the defart Glade,
Fair to no purpofe, flatter'd Graces fade!—
One healing draught—and all fhall yet be well!
" Peace is the pale-ey'd Sifter of the Cell,"
The cell of DEATH—where Mifery only knows
The foft exemption,—and the long repofe.

Ah no!—a guardian Spirit feems to fay,
" Stay thee, Louisa, yet a little ftay!
" Awake not righteous Heaven's avenging Hate
" By rafhly plunging in the waves of Fate!
" Tho' Time, for wóes like thine, admits no cure,
" Yet learn its hardeft leffon, to endure!
" Not long fhall life her torturing fenfe impart
" Of the barb'd fhaft, that rankles in thy heart.
" Thou fhalt not need to ftain thy fpotlefs Soul,
" Nor want th' enfanguin'd knife, th' envenom'd bowl;
                                        " Thy

" Thy Soul's Belov'd, by vain ambition fired,

" Deaf, as the Grave, to all that once infpired,

" To Love's foft voice,—to Honor's awful plea,

" Lives to another!—and is loft to thee!"

EUGENIO *married!*—Oh!—yon Village-bell,

That flings on the cold Gale its mournful knell!

The folemn paufe,—the loud repeated toll,

Calling the pale Corfe to its darkfome goal,

Not plainer there the tale of Death relate,

Than thefe detefted words pronounce my fate!

EUGENIO *married*, feals LOUISA's doom,

Her fure, tho' lingering pafsport to the tomb!

And thou, foft Mourner o'er my bofom's fmart!

Friend of my Soul, and Sifter of my Heart!

A fallen Bloffom while thy tears embalm,

Regrets that Fondnefs prompts, let Fondnefs calm;

Since tho' this mortal Frame, Affection's flave,

Waftes by th' envenom'd wound that Falfehood gave,

I ftill poffefs, thus withering in my youth,

The peace of Innocence, the pride of Truth;

E   My

My Soul is confcious of its heavenly Sire,
The Cherub Faith has lent her wings of fire;
Man, the bafe object of my fcorn, it leaves,
To join that gracious Power, that ne'er deceives!

When bufy Rumours to thy ear difclofe
The long enfranchifement of all my woes,
Oh! let thy Mind's pure eye behold me foar
Where Light, and Life from Springs unfailing pour!
Mark the bright circlets of th' eternal Morn,
In radiant points, my fmiling brows adorn!
By kindred Seraphs fee thy Friend embraced,
Not one flight thought on falfe EUGENIO wafte!
Yet, tho' from Pain, and Grief for ever free,
Throw back foft Pity's tender glance on thee!
Smile at the human weaknefs of thy tears,
And long to welcome thee to HAPPIER SPHERES!

END OF THE FIRST EPISTLE.

E U G E N I O

T O

E M M A,

ON HER RETURN FROM THE EAST-INDIES.

APRIL 15, 1781.

START not, dear E M M A, at an haplefs name,
Veil'd to thy fenfe in perfidy and fhame!
Oh! deep indeed the mifts, they long have fpread,
To Fancy's eye, round this devoted head!
While deeper ftill the fhades of anguifh lower,
Drear as the Night upon the wintry Bower,
When bitter Winds howl fearful o'er the plains,
And the bright Stars are quench'd amid the rains!

E 2

So

So quench'd each smiling Pleasure's roseate ray,
That once illumin'd lost Eugenio's way!

But, e'er his tortur'd Soul's incessant strife
Burst the dark confines of disastrous Life,
Given, or with-held, by Emma's guardian hands,
As her Friend's peace hereafter best demands,
Will she receive Eugenio's last request,
In faithful trust for her Louisa's breast,
Hear his sad story—that yet dares appear
To claim her justice, and implore her tear?

If so, let now thy gentle heart incline
To mourn the trials, and the pangs of mine!
No longer shalt thou think I basely sold
My peace, my liberty, my love, for gold;
That gold did purchase them, we know too well,
But Oh! no *sordid* sacrifice they fell!
Learn then those dire Events, whose tyrant sway
Forc'd me to throw joy's vital root away,
Yield my Louisa to their stern controul,
Gem of my youth! and day-star of my soul!

To

To thee, fo long accuftom'd to difclofe
Whate'er on Life the ftrengthen'd colour throws,
To thee Louisa queftionlefs appeal'd;
Reveal'd my vows, my broken faith reveal'd;
Taught thee, thro' fcenes, now paft and gone, to rove,
And hate the mean apoftate to his love.

Veil'd by her native Groves, I left the Maid,
And journied onward from that blooming Glade,
With eyes, full oft reverted as I pafs'd,
With many a look to Heaven in fervor caft,
To implore protection for Louisa's peace,
Her health's dear fafety, and our love's increafe.

E'er yet I join'd the animated Train,
Whofe full-fraught Veffels feek the ports of Gain,
To that domeftic fcene I bent my way,
Which far in * Deva's woodland mazes lay;

* The River Deva, celebrated by Milton, and other of our Poets, rifes in Merioneth-
fhire, and flows thro' mountainous and beautiful fcenery, ftill, as it is faid, retaining its
original name. In Chefhire it affumes that of Dee, which led fome of the Commentators
on the firft Edition of this Poem to fuppofe the Villa of Ernefto in that county; but the
author meant to place it in Wales, on the banks of the Deva, before it changes its title
for one fo much lefs harmonious, and waters a country more fertile, but much lefs lovely.

A rural

A rural kind Retreat from all the cares,
Which bufy Commerce for her Sons prepares.
Tranflucent Deva the green Valley laves,
And darkling Alders fcreen her wandering waves,
Till flow fhe rifes from o'er-hanging Shades,
And, feen at diftance, thro' the opening Glades,
With bank lefs veil'd, and ftreams that mildly fhine,
Leads round the lonely Hills her filver line.

In that fweet Dale, and by a Mountain's fide,
Whofe fheltering heights the angry North deride,
Abode, fo late, of Cheerfulnefs and Eafe,
White gleams the Manfion thro' the waving Trees!
Tall are the Trees that whifper round its Walls,
And foft the pathway down the Valley falls!
Oh! how each charm, that decks the quiet fcene,
Affum'd new grace, and wore a fofter mein,
From the bleft thought, that foon the nuptial Hour
Would lead LOUISA to my native bower!

'Twas there my gentle Parents often knew
The calm fweet Night, the Day that lightly flew;

And

And there the heart-felt pleafure gaily fhew'd
EUGENIO's welcome to the green abode.
A Father's elevating gladnefs proved
How dear the prefence of the Son he loved.
My gentle Mother, archly fmiling, preft
The love-fick Wanderer to her honor'd breaft;
For fo fhe fondly call'd her darling Youth,
Yet lov'd his ardor, and approv'd his truth.
My Sifters, fair, ingenuous, graceful Maids,
Th' acknowledg'd pride of all the neighbouring Shades,
Met me with bounding ftep, and joyous mein,
And rays of tranfport brightened all the fcene.

Nor wilt thou, mighty Love! upbraid my Heart,
For bearing in their joys fo warm a part;
Since no ambition gloom'd my Father's brow,
No thirft of wealth reproach'd my plighted vow;
He fcorn'd to name LOUISA's want of gold,
But gladly liftened while her worth I told.
Pleas'd has he feen her in this melting eye,
Pleas'd with her name, half whifpered in a figh;

Then

Then would I grafp his hand, and ardent fay,

" Oft fhall my Parents blefs our bridal Day,

" Since from that Soul of fweetnefs, they fhall fhare

" A Daughter's tendernefs, an Angel's care;

" For her's each Virtue, and each Grace refin'd,

" That breathe on Lovelinefs the glow of Mind,

" And, with affiduous Duty's cheering pow'r,

" Strew Life's worn path with ev'ry filial flow'r."

One Eve, as on the fhady bank I rode,

Where thro' new Dales the beauteous Deva flow'd,

Loitering I liften to the Red-breaft clear,

The laft, lone Songfter of the waining Year.

Light o'er the leaves fweet Autumn breathes ferene,

And tips with gold their yet unfaded green.

Now many a vapor grey the ftream exhales,

And Twilight fteals unheeded on the Vales;

O'er the hill-top the lines of crimfon run,

The glowing raiments of the vanifh'd Sun;

Nor yet the deep'ning fhades of Night impede

My roving courfe, which penfive mufings lead,

What

What time the *Moon of Ceres mildly throws
Her fhadowy grace, and breathes her foft repofe
O'er the dark Shrubs, that clothe the rocky Steeps,
Shelve from their tops, and fringe the cryftal Deeps;
While, as around thofe Rocks the River glides,
White moon-beams tremble in the glancing tides.

Sudden, wild founds are borne along the gales!
The piercing fhriek my ftartled ear affails!
But fcarce a moment, with check'd rein, I ftand,
Th' uplifted cane grafp'd fternly in my hand,
E'er bending forward o'er my eager Horfe,
Urging, with needlefs fpur, his rapid courfe,
And plunging thro' the deep, oppofing flood,
I pierce the tangled mazes of the Wood.
On fibrous Oaks, that roughen all the ground,
My Steed's fleet hoofs, with hollow noife, refound;
And doubled by the echos from the caves,
Appal a guilty band of defperate Slaves;
For foon, in ruthlefs, felon-gripe, I found
A beauteous Female, fcreaming on the ground;

* *Moon of Ceres*, the Harveft Moon.

F

Dragg'd

Dragg'd from her Horfe, that graz'd unconfcious near,
Her treffes torn, and frantic with her fear.
Two liveried Youths, attendant on the Maid,
At the firft onfet in that gloomy Glade,
Had, or feduced by Gold, or wing'd by dread,
From danger, and from duty, coward fled.

Alarm'd, the Villains quit their ftruggling Prey,
And two, with terror ftruck, fpeed faft away.
Fiercer the third, the arm of blood extends;
The levell'd tube, in dire direction, bends!
Yet no cold fear arrefts my vengeful force,
And his wing'd death-ball flies with erring courfe;
But not defcends my nervous blow in vain,
The hidden lead indents the Murderer's brain;
With one demoniac glance, as down he fell,
The Soul ftarts furious from its vital cell.

Then tender pity, and affiduous care,
Conduct me fwiftly to the fwooning Fair.
The light, cool drops, fcoop'd from the neighbouring fpring,
O'er her pale brow folicitous I fling;

Till

Till Life's warm tide, which long the Heart detains,
Returns, flow purpling the forsaken veins.

In one deep figh, as Recollection came,
It wakens Gratitude's impetuous flame.

" For more than Life," exclaims the trembling Maid,
" I ftand indebted to thy generous aid."

' Ceafe, Fair-One, ceafe.—well might this arm deferve
' That deadlieft Palfies wither ev'ry nerve,
' Had it refus'd the aid to thee it gave,
' Or coward fhunn'd the duty of the Brave!
' But let me now, fince danger haunts delay,
' To fafer fcenes my lovely Charge convey.
' Deep in yon vale, ERNESTO's modeft Dome
' Lifts its fair head—my tranquil, happy home!
' There ev'ry welcome fhall her fteps receive,
' That hofpitable affluence knows to give.'

This faid, her trembling Form, with anxious hafte,
My twining arms on her light Courfer placed ;

F 2   Then,

Then, as emerging from the darkling Wood,
Along the moon-bright Dales we flowly rode,
Surpris'd his gorgeous trappings I behold,
The net of Silver, and the thongs of gold;
While all the veftments of the lovely Dame
The pride of elevated rank proclaim.
The coftly lace had golden leaves imprest
Light on the borders of the pearly veft;
Her taper waift the broider'd zone entwines,
Clafp'd by a Gem, the boaft of Orient Mines;
On as we pafs, on ev'ry fide it gleams,
And to the Moon, in trembling luftre, ftreams!

Dear E m m a, that the fplendid garb could gain,
E'en in an hour exempt from grief and pain
Th' attentive gaze, proves my devoted heart
From eyes fo bright met no refiftlefs dart;
For when the Maid Love's potent ceftus wears,
The jealous God no glance dividual bears.

Ah! in thofe halcyon days, a Mind at eafe
Empower'd flight things to intereft, and to pleafe;

That

That Memory fhould their faded tints relume,
When Deprivation's deepeft fhadows gloom,
Perhaps feems ftrange!—but now, that full, and free,
My long imprifon'd Spirit fprings to thee,
Friend of my Love! to whom I dare reveal
All that my Soul has felt, or knows to feel,
So foften'd feem th' afperities of Grief,
My Senfes anchor on the kind relief;
With trivial circumftance retard the pen,
E'er languid Solitude fhall lower again;
For oh! when loft in woes of lengthen'd date,
Alone we've lean'd upon the thorn of Fate,
Seeking, at laft, the kind affuafive reft,
Found only on Compaffion's downy breaft,
We feel, as foft th' imparted Sorrows flow,
Almoft difcharg'd the bitternefs of Woe.

Within ERNESTO's hofpitable gates,
Alarm'd at my delay, Affection waits;
But as I lead the bright diftinguifh'd Maid,
Explain her danger, and my profperous aid,

The

The dear Inhabitants around her move,
With deep refpect, kind care, and generous love.

And foon we learn, our peaceful walls contain
The fplendid Heirefs of a vaft Domain,
EMIRA, fhe, whofe wealth, and charms infpire,
The croud of titled Youth with amorous fire;
While Rumour paints her, 'midft th' obfequious Train,
Tho' frolic, infolent; tho' haughty, vain.
But to our eyes, thefe wild and wandering fires
Are fcreen'd by rifing Hopes, and gay Defires;
For ftill, the parting Hour with care delay'd,
EMIRA loiters in ERNESTO's fhade;
The noon-tide Sun, the Evening's fofter ray
Beholds the Fair-One thro' the Valley ftray;
Thus, on * MATILDA leaning, fondly own
Her Heart's new choice in Paffion's warmeft tone.

" Loft to the World, for ever could I dwell
" In the dear precincts of this fylvan Cell;

* EUGENIO's Sifter.

" Renounce

" Renounce each vain, tho' once ador'd delight,
" That diffipates the Day, or gilds the Night;
" That can each gay feducing art employ,
" To flatter Beauty, and infpirit Joy."

Thus the proud Maid, of all her fcorn difarm'd,
By ftrange, and partial preference ftrongly charm'd,
Feels a new Eden fteal upon the bowers,
And chides with fighs the fwiftly fleeting Hours;
Still at the cheerful Board, or as fhe roves
Along the Plain, or lingers in the Groves,
Each glowing wifh, from new-born Paffion fprung,
Each foft diforder, on her eye-lids hung,
At my approach reveal, tho' much in vain,
What words are little wanted to explain.
Vain! had I never feen the matchlefs grace,
The touching fweetnefs of LOUISA's face;
Where from each feature beams, or mildly plays,
Refined intelligence, with varying rays;
Where native dignity, with air ferene,
Confcious, not arrogant, adorns her mein;

While

While from thofe eyes, in fcorn of artful wiles,
The tender fpotlefs Soul looks out, and fmiles.——
Thefe unbeheld, yet ftill EMIRA's charms
Had ne'er allur'd EUGENIO to her arms;
For oh! the fever'd languor of the eye,
The reftlefs blufhes, the voluptuous figh,
Th' impatient haughtinefs, but half conceal'd,
The rage of pleafure in each glance reveal'd,
Tho' in youth's fervid hours, perchance they fire
The kindling ardours of unaw'd Defire,
Quench, while the tranfient flames their force impart,
The torch of Paffion, e'er it reach the Heart.

'Twas thus the youthful Ithacan furvey'd
The Goddefs Nymph, beneath her magic Shade;
While Eucharis' mild beauties foil'd the fway
Of charms, that deck'd the Daughter of the Day;
By Love protected, when the Princely Boy
Beheld the Dame her wonted lures employ;
Saw her fine Form, by all the Graces dreft,
The glowing purple of the floating veft,

And

And on her blooming cheek the treſſes bright,
That play'd in wavy wreaths of golden light,
Or on her ſnowy boſom, ſhining fell,
Like a warm Sun-beam on a Lilly's bell.

Not more EMIRA's charms my Soul engage,
The fair Calypſo of a ſenſual age ;
And than licentious Beauty leſs, the ſtores
That ſplendid Fortune on EMIRA pours ;
Or the proud boaſt of lineal Blood, allied
To Rank, and Pow'r, could wake that ſenſeleſs Pride,
Which quenches the ſoft warmth that Love inſpires,
And lights the nuptial torch with rayleſs fires.

To ſave the Fair-One from the thorny ſmart
Of hopeleſs Paſſion, rankling in her heart,
I urge my gentle Siſters to reveal
All my charm'd ſenſes for LOUISA feel ;
The worth, the graces, which around her wait,
And all the ſmiling proſpect of our fate.

G   EMIRA

Emira liftens with impaffion'd fcorn,
Of wounded Pride, and rival Anger born.
Unwifh'd, unwelcome, as the theme arofe,
Her clouded cheek in deep fuffufion glows,
Proudly exclaiming,—"Can Eugenio prove
" Cold, and obdurate to my lavifh Love?
" Has Beauty's magic zone my bofom bound,
" Does Rank exalt me, and has Fortune crown'd,
" That faint attractions in a Village Maid
" Should fhield the Paffions which thefe eyes invade?
" Impoffible!—but oh! thy lips impart
" The fting of jealoufy, that goads my heart.
" Matilda, all my waking dreams divine
" Thy charming Brother fhall at length be mine!
" This groveling flame was but ordain'd to prove
" Thy Friend's wifh'd triumph at the fhrine of Love,
" And by comparifon of brighter charms,
" To light Eugenio to Emira's arms."

Thus, while felf-flatt'ring Pride her Mind affures,
The artful Fair-One fpreads her varied lures;

Sometimes,

Sometimes, with archnefs laughing in her eyes,
Hangs on my arm, and ridicules my fighs;
And oft with coyer tendernefs appears,
While Love's warm glances fteal thro' fhining tears;
Now, with arch'd brow, and fupercilious ftare,
Affects the emprefs-dignity of air;
And now, as reafoning with a wayward Heart,
In trances, broken by the frequent ftart,
With paufing ftep fhe wanders thro' the Grove,
A female Proteus in the wiles of Love!

To mufe at leifure on my lovely Maid,
And woo her image in the lonely Glade,
Where no EMIRA, by the rigid laws
Politenefs dictates, my attention draws,
Far in the Wilds I wander thro' the Day,
And to a lowly Cot at midnight ftray;
There tafte the fweetnefs of that deep repofe,
Which from applauding Confcience gently flows,
When Health, and Hope their downy pinions fpread,
And fcatter rofes on the youthful bed.

Light

Light with the Dawn difperfe my tender dreams ;
And now the Sun looks golden on the ftreams !—
O Morn ! the laft for me that gaily rofe,
On Memory's tablet ftill thy beauty glows.
Charm'd, as I wander'd thro' the dewy Vale,
And drank the fpirit of the Mountain-gale,
How little did my unconfcious heart divine,
The joys thou gav'ft fhould ne'er again be mine !

On as I rov'd along the winding Glades,
A Youth in hafte the fylvan Copfe pervades !
Says, his commiffion inftantly recalls
My devious ftep to the paternal walls.
Upon the ruftic countenance appears
A fix'd folemnity, that wakes my fears.—
" Oh ! is all well ?"—with breathlefs hafte I cry,
" Thy Friends are well,"—his faltering lips reply ;
Then dread, left fad intelligence invade
The precious quiet of my native Shade,
Sickens my heart ;—and fwiftly as I go,
From my pale lip diforder'd accents flow ;

Each

Each moment, for LOUISA's Life, arife
Prayers, that implore the mercies of the Skies.

And now my quick, unequal fteps are led,
A Day of gladnefs where they us'd to fpread;
But ah! no filver tones EUGENIO call!
No bounding foot-ftep meets me in the hall!
Sufpenfe, with all its heavy heart-ach, teems,
And palpable the folemn ftillnefs feems!

So, when returning from the well-fought plain,
As near thy Caftle-walls thou led'ft thy Train,
O * Hardiknute! fuch pangs as thefe oppreft,
In Hope's warm hour, thy brave, and veteran breaft.
Along the midnight glooms, that thick impend,
While howls the Storm, the beating Rains defcend,
Thou fee'ft no Guard upon thy turrets height,
Whofe ftreaming torches us'd to gild the night!
Black, as a mourning weed, they filent ftand,
And daunt the ftouteft heart in Scotia's Land!

* See the admired fcotch fragment, HARDIKNUTE, in Percy's collection of ancient poetry.

Appall'd,

Appall'd, like him, I felt the ſtillneſs dire;
Eager to learn—not daring to enquire,
As one transfix'd, a few dread minutes wait,
While ſilent Horror ſhrouds impending Fate!

My Father enter'd—with a cheek how pale!
And oh! that look!—it told an awful tale!
'Twas mournful!—ſupplicating!—" Heavenly Powers!
" In that dim gaze how deep an anguiſh lowers!
" Louisa! lives ſhe?"—dreading the reply,
My Soul hung trembling in my ſtraining eye.

" My Son, the ſweet Louisa lives,—and knows,
" I hope, the peace that Innocence beſtows;
" Oh! may it long be her's!—but now remains
" A taſk for me, replete with ſharpeſt pains!—
" Eugenio!—Penury's dire blaſts aſſail,
" And Hope is frozen in the bitter gale!
" Yes,—Belmor has deceiv'd my boundleſs truſt,
" To Friendſhip treacherous, and to Faith unjuſt!
" Unhappy Hour, when Confidence intire
" Lur'd me to follow that miſleading fire,

" Thoſe

" Thofe gay commercial vifions, falfe, and vain,
" The glittering meteors of his artful brain !
" Too well he knew no genuine light they gave,
" And now they fink in Ruin's whelming wave !

" Oh ! great, and numberlefs the Ills, that fpread
" Their mingled horrors round this aged head !
" The pang of feeing thy fweet Sifters, born
" To faireft hopes, from eafe, and affluence torn !
" Expos'd to all thofe guileful fnares, that wait
" The beauteous Indigent's difaftrous fate !
" Ills, whofe bare dread a Father's bofom tears,
" And blends with agony his anxious cares.
" Thy dearer Mother !"—Here he turn'd his head
And paufing wept ;—at length refuming, faid,

" Thefe hovering woes, that o'er our houfe impend,
" Thou, my dear Son, e'er their dread weight defcend,
" Thou canft avert !—but oh ! at what a price !
" Perfuafion fhall not urge—nor prayers intice.

" Two

" Two hours e'er thy return, EMIRA found
" Thy Sifters eyes in ftreaming torrents drown'd ;
" Learn'd, from their trembling lips, the cruel Caufe,
" Which the dark cloud of confternation draws
" Wide o'er my Roof—that yefterday furvey'd,
" Domeftic Comfort's fair, and favorite fhade.

" We know that Fortune on EMIRA pours
" Her golden treafures in unftinted fhowers.—
" EUGENIO!—fhe ftands ready to replace
" Thy Father's comforts on a lafting bafe!
" Refcue his falling Fame!—the numbers fave,
" Whofe hopes in his deftruction find a grave;
" And light, while Woe's dark cloud her wealth removes,
" Joy's living fpark in many an eye he loves!
" But at the price—Great God!—thy Father's fears
" Shrink from the found, and whelm it with his tears!
" By fharp Diftrefs at laft to name it driven!—
" Thy hand to her,—e'en at the ALTAR given!—
" Alas! th' impoffibility e'en now
" Glooms in the grief, the horror of thy brow!—

                                        " Oh!

" Oh ! for *myself*—I could not wish to gain
" Exemption from the sharpest earthly pain,
" By banishing each hope, his Love had won,
" From the kind, duteous bosom of my Son !
" But for their dearer sakes who fall with me,
" Perhaps I dare—to hope e'en *this* from thee.

" Thou know'st, when Peace, and Plenty's jocund Powers
" Hung their ripe clusters round our blooming bowers,
" The joys that Love, not those which Wealth impart,
" Form'd the warm wish for thee, that fill'd my heart ;
" But now—EUGENIO listen !—could'st thou bear
" LOUISA's breast this weight of woes should share ?
" Would'st thou the blossoms of her youth transplant
" Into the blasting soil of worldly Want ?
" Whose pangs, tho' ne'er her soft complaints reveal,
" She will not therefore less severely feel ;
" Since when a breast, far dearer than our own,
" Receives the darts by that fell Demon thrown,
" Fast wasting health, and spirits broke, will prove,
" Far from extracted, they are barb'd by Love."

H   Here

Here fighs, that feem'd to fhake his frame, betray'd
How deep he felt the forrows he pourtray'd;
But yet, tho' ftill his heart with anguifh bled,
Fail'd fpeech recovering foon, again he faid,

" It is not much my waining Life's remains
" Should fhorten'd fink by Penury's cruel pains ;
" Ah! rather could I bear their utmoft ftrife,
" Than wifh to quench the torch that gilds thy Life,
" Sweet *Poffibility!* which yet appears,
" Borne on th' eventful flight of days, and years,
" Whofe chance propitious might each bar remove
" Or Induftry reftore the joys of Love ;
" Tho' fharp the confcioufnefs, that BELMOR's art
" Muft to my Fame the deadlieft wound impart !
" For oh! the Many, who their ruin owe
" To my rafh hopes unhappy overthrow,
" Will, without fcruple, think by fraud I won
" The confidence, which drew that ruin on.

" Hard to refign, for fuch opprobrious blame,
" The honeft triumph of a fpotlefs name ;

" E'en

" E'en when the Heart dares to itfelf appeal

" From blind Injuftice, and mifguided Zeal!

" Their torrent Reafon ftrives to ftem in vain,

" Truth pleads to Air, if Prejudice arraign.

" Her cenfures daily level with the Bafe

" A thoufand names, no actual crimes difgrace;

" Pull down the fame a Life of virtue built,

" And ftamp Imprudence with the brand of Guilt.

" And yet, I would not afk my Child to fave

" From Pains, that feem to rob of reft the *Grave*,

" My haplefs Spirit, at a price fo great,

" To fhade perchance with deeper gloom his fate!

" But, oh! my lov'd EUGENIO!—from a woe,

" Sharper, I truft, than thou wilt ever know,

" My Senfe recoils!—my Wife!—my deareft Wife!

" The fweet Companion of my lengthen'd Life!

" Thy Mother!—for whofe peace, and health, my cares,

" My fond attention, my inceffant prayers

" The Day, and Night beheld!—Oh! muft I fee

" That dear One pine in helplefs Poverty?

" While pale, and trembling, finks the vital flame,

" Muft her foft, delicate, and feeble Frame,

" To

" To Charity's donation, cold, and scant,

" Owe its exemption from extremest want?

" Can I see this—unable to obtain

" Those common comforts the *Laborious* gain,

" Conscious, my own infatuated rashness shed

" This bitter phial on her gentle head?

'" My Son!—my Son!"—Then, on my shoulder thrown,

Heart-smote, and wan, he heav'd the bitter groan.

Oh! while these arms their honour'd Burden prest,

As his sunk cheek felt cold upon my breast,

What words can paint the deep distress I bore,

What Horror smote me, and what Anguish tore?

And could I see the Author of my birth

Thus bend in woe the hoary head to Earth;

Round his weak Frame such whelming anguish rage,

Nor snatch from the dread storm his failing age,

Because my Hopes—my Peace—perhaps my Life

Were doom'd to perish in the filial strife?

Impossible!—the softer Passions fly,

Nor dare dissolve great Nature's primal tie.

" Be

" Be comforted, my Father !—could thy Son,
" Oh ! could he live to fee thee thus undone,
" Endure the knowledge, that when Fortune gave
" The power to fave thee, he refus'd to fave ?
" The torturing felf-reproach muft rend his brain,
" And wake to phrenzy the remorfeful pain.
" But O my Love !—yet pardon me !—I go
" Alone to ftem conflicting tides of woe !
" I go, to teach my Soul her arduous tafk,
" And gain by prayer the fortitude I afk !"

So faying, to his couch my Sire I led,
And fmooth'd the pillow for his languid head.
With fofter tears his trembling eye-balls fhone,
And faltering accents ardent bleft his Son.

Then up the Mountain's fteep, and craggy fide,
With ftep precipitate, I wildly ftride ;
Now ftung with tortures of the laft defpair ;
Now funk in grief ;—now energiz'd by prayer ;
Nor yet in vain th' heart rending efforts prove,
Warm Duty rifes over bleeding Love !

The

The ſtruggle paſt!—my peace!—my freedom given!
Thy anchor Hope, on ſhorelefs oceans driven!
What then to Juſtice, or to Love remain'd,
But to reſtore the heart, my vows had gain'd?
Wrench from Louiſa's breaſt its cheriſh'd bane,
And nobly the laſt ſacrifice ſuſtain?
Renounce her pity, and inſpire her hate,
In tenfold gloom, tho' it involve my fate?
Teach her to think the Villain-baſeneſs mine,
That bows the venal Heart at Fortune's ſhrine?
So might th' indignant ſenſe of barter'd Truth
Quench the difaſtrous Paſſion of her Youth;
Now doom'd to darken every Hope, that cheers,
With ſhining promifes, the rifing years!
Had I the dread neceſſity explain'd,
That with refiſtlefs force my freedom chain'd;
Tore the fweet bands, by virtuous Paſſion tied,
And ſtamp'd our Conſtancy with Paricide;
Then had Louiſa fortified my Soul,
And urg'd my ling'ring ſtep to Duty's goal;
Had given me back, with Pity's ſofteſt brow,
Of Love ſo ruinous, the ill-ſtarr'd vow;

A ſelf-

A felf-devoted Exile fled my arms,
But forrowing fled them, and refign'd her charms
To fruitlefs Conftancy, and fond Regret;
Ordain'd to mourn—unable to forget;
That pine in Solitude the live-long Day,
Feed on the heart, and fteal the life away.

Louisa's pity had my fufferings found,
Somewhat it fure had balm'd th' embofom'd wound;
But fince e'en her dear fympathy was weak,
Of Fate's dread fhaft th' envenom'd point to break,
I ftrove to avert the flow-confuming pain,
And for the conflict, arm'd her with difdain;
That cruel conflict, which the Paffions prove,
E'er high-foul'd Scorn fubdues a rooted Love.

Still, to my Being's lateft verge, be borne
The dear, miftaken Maid's unceafing fcorn;
Oh! be they borne in this unhappy breaft,
To the cold bed of its eternal reft!

Near

Near feems that reft my wearied Life defires,
Pain breaks her fprings, and Sicknefs dims her fires,
And Hope, who comes in fable veft array'd,
Points, with pale hand, to Death's eternal fhade!

But yet,—when paft the expiatory doom,
When Mifery's fhafts lie broken on my tomb,
Th' exploring gaze, fweet E M M A, kindly bend
On the dear bofom of thy beauteous Friend ;
If thou fhalt mark, that cold contempt fuftains
That feat of foftnefs from affaulting Pains ;
That no dim tears her check's warm rofes pale,
No fighs of anguifh fwell the lonely gale,
Whofe murmurs o'er the grafs-green fod fhall rife,
Where, cold, and peaceful, loft E U G E N I O lies,
Then, that thou name me *not*, my Soul implores,
Nor fnatch the peace away Difdain reftores ;
The cruel change thy tendernefs will fear,
Of Pride's ftern frown, for Pity's heart-wrung tear.
Oh! fhall one felfifh wifh her peace invade
That Love fo agoniz'd may footh my fhade ?

No,

No, EMMA, no!—my Soul for her's fhall wait,
Till foft it pafs the everlafting Gate;
From thofe dear Eyes till Light Divine fhall clear,
The film, that mortal Chance had darken'd there;
Fond Memory's deep reproach for aye remove,
And pleading Seraphs reunite our Love!

But Oh! fhould Pity, with intrufive fway,
Range her fad Images in dire array,
And to LOUISA's mental fight difclofe
The bed of Death—the agonizing throes;
Oh! fhould fhe think fhe fees in ftruggles rife
That breath, which wak'd for her the fondeft fighs!
Thofe Eyes, whofe foftnefs fhall no more betray,
Throw their laft glances on the final day!—
In fuch an hour, fhould Scorn, and Anger prove
Weak to difpel the grief-awaken'd 'Love;
Sorrowing for him, who could her hopes deceive,
Should fhe, in bitternefs of Spirit, grieve
For Guilt, which, unextenuated, rears
Barriers to laft beyond this Vale of tears;
Then, EMMA, then, the fad events relate,
That wove the fable texture of our fate.

I

My

My dear Louisa!—pardon him, who ſtrove
By means, ſo ſeeming harſh, to quench thy Love !
Hard was the taſk, that kindneſs to reſign,
Which my torn boſom could demand of thine ;
Eſteem, that might have borne eternal date,
Since placed, by Virtue, paſt the reach of Fate ;
That bleſs'd compaſſion, my ſad lot had won,
A Wretch by Fortune, not by Crimes undone ;
Theſe to renounce !—with my own hand to throw
In her dark chalice added dregs of woe ;
To pierce my Soul with voluntary pains,
A Suicide on Comfort's laſt remains,
Was hard !—but generous Love the effort made,
Thy quiet aſk'd ;—I trembled—and obey'd !

When to that purer World our Souls are borne,
Where every veil from every breaſt is torn,
My willing Spirit, in the Realms above,
Shall meet the ſearching Eye of wounded Love ;
To thee Louisa my paſt woes impart,
And hear thy Angel Voice ABSOLVE MY HEART.

END OF THE SECOND EPISTLE.

L O U I S A

TO

E M M A,

WRITTEN THE DAY AFTER SHE HAD RECEIV'D FROM HER
EUGENIO's EXCULPATING LETTER.

APRIL 21ft, 1781.

O! Thou foft Hope, that once with luftre gay
    Did'ft gild the hours of Love's delicious day,
What, tho' no more the lively joy remains,
That traced thy light ftep o'er thefe earthly plains,
Yet, piercing now Defpair's incumbent fhroud,
Soft Hope, thou lookeft from yon parting cloud;
And my lov'd EMMA's hand the vifion fhews,
That fmiles my ftruggling Spirit to repofe!
Bright in EUGENIO's vindicated truth,
That vifion lights anew my drooping youth;

I 2

For,

For, in perspective beauteous, it displays
A long eternity of blissful days;
Of all those sacred joys our Souls shall prove
" When pleading Seraphs reunite our love."

'Tis true, Eugenio, thro' Life's thorny way,
In far divided paths our steps shall stray;
It is not given us, when rude blasts assail,
And pale Misfortune breathes the bitter gale,
It is not given, to temper, and assuage,
Each for the other's breast, its cruel rage;
Nor mutually to feel the cheering rays,
When Health, and Joy inspirit Summer-days.
Our little Barks, their flattering Port in view,
Fate, on Life's billowy surge, asunder threw;
Friend of my soul! we are not doom'd to gain
The sunny Isle of that tempestuous Main;
But O! thy Virtue, long imagin'd lost,
Has felt the wreck of no insiduous coast!
The deep and troubled floods, it knew to brave!
It rises buoyant on the stormy waves!

Vain

Vain are thofe Storms, by which its courfe is driven,
Since fure, tho' diftant, is the port of Heaven.

My dear EUGENIO, the dread Voice will prove
.Indulgent to the frail excefs of Love,
Which to fuch fad extremes would blindly run,
Lavifh of health, and fickening at the Sun ;
Since, while an unaccufing Confcience threw
Th' eternal portals open to my view,
My Spirit funk, a prey to fond Defpair,
And coldly view'd that Heaven thou could'ft not fhare ;
Soil'd with its griefs thofe amaranthine flowers,
Inwove by Faith in bright Religion's bowers.
Angel of Mercy ! thou wilt gently breathe
Exhaling fighs upon that fullied wreath ;
And the dim ftains of my impatient tears,
Impaffion'd yearnings, and defponding fears,
Shall vanifh, as chill dews that Morning throws,
By Summer Winds are wafted from the Rofe !

O ! how o'er-joy'd my dazzled fight furvey'd
Thefe words, in EMMA's characters pourtray'd,

" He

" He is not guilty!"—rapid from my tongue
They, in exulting iteration, fprung.
" Read, dear Louisa, and acquit the Heart,
" That bears in all thy griefs fo large a Part."

Think'ft thou, my Emma, thy benign command
Met an unwilling eye, a tardy hand?
Heaven! with what force thefe hands, thefe eyes, impell'd,
Seize the known charaĉters, fo long with-held!
While every letter, e'er examin'd, wears
Th' uninjur'd magic of the vanifh'd years!
Diforder'd founds my lips pronounce, nor fpare
The ufelefs queftion to th' unconfcious air.
" Does that dear hand yet trace Louisa's name?
" Will it his Love, his Innocence proclaim?
" How may this be?—yet Emma fays 'tis fo."
Then did I read, and weep, and throb, and glow,
Approve, abfolve, admire, and fmile, and figh,
Till penfive Peace fhone mildly in my eye;
Back with that loft efteem, my heart deplor'd,
The Wanderer came, with half her rights reftor'd.

So

So lucklefs CLAIRMONT's thorny path fhe fmooths;
So his fharp fenfe of many an ill fhe fooths;
One dear recover'd Hope his grief beguiles,
And, 'midft the wreck of all the reft, he fmiles.
EMMA, thou knew'ft him well;—the jocund Youth,
Ambition's Votary, yet of taintlefs truth.
Lur'd by the wealth the glowing Andes hide,
He long'd to pafs the interpofing tide.
Remembrance fees him on the Sea-beach ftand,
His fair CLARISSA weeping on his hand.
With anxious fmiles her varying cheek he dries,
And talks of profperous Winds, and favoring Skies.
Clear was the Sky, and gentle were the Gales,
And wide and waving ftream'd the fnowy Sails;
While, toffing the green fea-weed o'er, and o'er,
Crept the hufh'd billow on the fhelly fhore;
Soft as th' autumnal breeze among the fheaves,
Or gently ruftling in the fallen leaves;
And rolling in blue Light the watery Way
With frofted filver feem'd bedropt, and gay.

Impatient

Impatient CLAIRMONT led his penſive Bride,
As ſlow ſhe ſcal'd the Veſſel's ſtately ſide.
So ſmooth the Seas, the tall Bark ſeem'd to ſleep,
While her gay Pennants ting'd the glaſſy Deep.
Day after Day mild Breezes freſhen'd round,
Till Skies alone the mighty Waters bound.

But now, far diſtant from Britannia's ſhore,
Round craggy Steeps where angry billows roar,
Riſe the dark Winds!—and borne on flagging wing,
On the bent maſt the ſcreaming Fulmars cling!
And ſoon the fury of the wildeſt Storm
That could the vext and ſwelling Sea deform,
With Death's ſhrill voice, ſhrieks in the rending ſhrouds,
As whirls the dizzy Veſſel to the clouds;
Or prone ſhoots ſwiftly to the billowy vale,
While the wet Seaman's altering cheek is pale.

The whirling Ship the guiding Rudder mocks,
It ſtrikes!—it burſts upon the bulging Rocks!
Unhappy CLAIRMONT, who had vainly tried
In the toſs'd Boat to place his beauteous Bride,

Sees,

Sees on the deck, pale, trembling, as she stood,
The sudden Billow dash her to the Flood;
While on the riven plank himself convey'd,
With only Life, beneath a stranger Shade,
Wakes from the briny trance, and wakes to know,
Of Fate's dark stores, the most accomplish'd Woe!
Borne by a friendly Sail, that now he stands
A ruin'd Wanderer on his native Lands,
Seems little ;—Love's severer tortures reign
With force despotic, and exclusive pain.

This borne, from month to month, and year to year,
At length, unlook'd for tidings charm his ear;
His fair CLARISSA lives!—on coasts unknown
Wreck'd, like himself, unfriended and alone,
By destiny severe, an hapless Slave,
Pines on rude shores beyond th' Atlantic wave;
Yet, that she *lives* is so unhoped a joy!—
Before it Doubt, and Fear, and Anguish fly!
She lives!—and Fate may aid the ardent strife,
And to his arms restore his long-lost Wife!

K

In

In that dear hope pale Mifery's tortures ceafe,
And agony fubfides almoft to peace.

So I—but to EUGENIO fwift impart
How full the pardon of LOUISA's heart!
O! let him not repent he wrung her Mind
With fruitlefs woes, fo generoufly defign'd;
Since, tho' they fail'd her freedom to reftore,
Had fhe not long been deftin'd to deplore
His Mind, as cruel, venal, falfe, and vain—
O but for that!—the Soul-diftracting pain,
Whofe unexpected flight makes other grief
Sink in the foftnefs of that bleft relief,
Her Spirit ne'er, as now, had rifen above
The poignant woes of difappointed Love;
Of that difunion here, ftern Fate commands,
Who throws her edicts with fuch ruthlefs hands!
But greater Ills remov'd, the lefs remain
Shorn of their pointed ftings, and loft their bane.
Say, in LOUISA's breaft no longer glow
The inward fires of life-confuming Woe;

Diftant

Diftant alike from Pain's incumbent gloom,
And fprightly Pleafure's gaily-kindling bloom,
The vital Powers effufe a fofter flame,
And with ferener beams pervade her Frame.
O bid him live!—live, to fulfil each part
That makes fuch awful claims upon his heart;
And as an Hufband, as a Father, prove
Virtuous, and great, as in his filial love!

I too fhall live!—Health's warmer currents break,
Yet unconfirm'd, upon my faded cheek,
Laft Night their honied dews prolong'd my reft,
As foft they fprung within my cherifh'd breaft.
O Night! the firft exempt from wildeft throes
Of fever'd Pain, that chas'd the fhort repofe,
Since my EUGENIO's feeming coldnefs ftrove,
Alas! how much in vain! to quench my Love.
Yes, I fhall live to expiate by a Mind
Bow'd to its fate, and cheerfully refign'd,
The dangerous rafhnefs, which my peace had thrown
On human chance, and errors not my own.

Here,

Here, to my favorite bower, at rifing Day,
With tranquil ftep, I bent my purpos'd way;
For here I firft beheld the graceful Youth,
And here he promis'd everlafting truth;
And here to thee, my Friend, I ufed to grieve,
When Life could charm no more, nor Hope deceive;
And here, my long afflicted Spirit, freed
From that barb'd fhaft, on which it wont to bleed,
Now bids its foften'd feelings gently flow,
To her, who draws the deadly fting of Woe.

Once more thefe eyes, with fmiles of pleafure hail
The vernal beauties of my native Vale;
The plenteous dews, that in the early ray
Gem the light leaf, and tremble on the fpray;
The frefh cool gales, that undulating pafs,
With fhadowy fweep, along the bending grafs.—
Now throw the fhrubs and trees the lengthen'd fhade
On the fmooth turf diftinct!—and now they fade,
As finks the Sun, behind a cloud withdrawn,
That late unveil'd fhone yellow on the lawn.

Soft

Soft o'er the Vale, from this my favorite feat,
Serene I mark the vagrant beauties fleet;
In different lights the changing features trace,
Catch the bright form, and paint the fhadowy grace.
Where the light Afh, and browner Oak extend,
And high in Air their mingled branches bend,
The mofly bank, beneath their trembling bowers,
Arifes, fragrant with uncultur'd flowers,
That ftoop the fweet head o'er the latent fpring,
And bear the pendant Bees, that humming cling.
Juft gleams the Fount—for, curving o'er its brink,
The lengthen'd grafs the fhining Waters drink;
Their green arms half its glafly beauties hide,
As from beneath them fteals the wandering tide,
And down the Valley carelefs winds away,
While in its ftreams the glancing Sun-beams play.

But where the Greenwood-hill, with arching fhade,
Opes the light Vifta up the winding Glade,
I fee a venerable Form defcend;
His flow fteps falter as they hither bend.

Soft

Soft lifts the breeze the locks of filver grey,
And gentleft meanings his mild looks convey!
Stranger, whoe'er thou art, thy faded face
And bending form have many a touching grace.
He ftops!——I haften to explore the caufe
Of that fix'd gaze!—of that impaffion'd paufe!

END OF THE THIRD EPISTLE.

NOTE, UPON reading this third Epiftle to a Friend, he obferved, that perhaps a comparifon of L o u i s a's own fituation with the harder fate of her Lover, and her tender pity for the inevitable miferies of fuch a union, might have been accept- able in the place of the epifode of C l a i r m o n t, and the defcription of the bower; but it fhould be confidered, that L o u i s a wrote under the immediate impreffion of her extacy to find E u g e n i o guiltlefs; that her Mind was not fober'd enough for reflection. To have inveftigated the unhappy lot of her Lover muft have been a melan- choly employment. Eafed of an oppreffive weight of mifery, her exhilarated fpirits admit not, fo early, any painful ideas. She does not difcriminate, fhe felicitates her deftiny. Her fympathy in the fate of her Friends grows more lively—fhe recollects the fituation of C l a i r m o n t—Joy is naturally loquacious, and fhe is gratified in relating his ftory to her E m m a. She awakens with new vivacity to the impreffions of pleafure, which her Mind was accuftomed to receive from fcenic objects. The propenfity to dwell on them prevailed even in the hours of her unhappinefs. It is an habit which compares and affimilates the fmiling, or the gloomy views of Nature to the internal feelings, and is common to people of a lively imagination. In the exultation of her Heart to find her Lover yet eftimable, L o u i s a fpeeds to the bower, fo imprefs'd with his image. Its beauties ftrike her more forcibly than ever, and in this frame of Mind fhe naturally feels delight in painting them.

FOURTH EPISTLE.

L O U I S A

T O

E M M A,

APRIL 25th, 1781.

OH! my lov'd EMMA, I have much to tell,
   Since laſt I ſent thee an abrupt farewel;
But be the chain of thoſe events regain'd,
That led my ſteps, where awful Horrors reign'd,
And thro' their gloom, the light of Joy reveal'd,
By Fate's eclipſing hand ſo long conceal'd.

   Riſing impatient from the moſſy ſeat,
With aſking eyes, the ſtranger Gueſt I meet;

                      He

He clasps my hand!—Oh! in that look benign,
What rays of love, and angel-pity shine!
Sweet cordial confidence my bosom cheers,
Yet thrilling start the soft spontaneous tears.

‘ What chance, or generous impulse, may I bless,
‘ Thrice gentle Stranger, for this kind address ;
‘ That thus thou visitest this lonely Grove,
‘ And gazest on me with paternal love ?’

“ Ah ! sweet Louisa,” the mild Form replies,
His words flow mingling with the rising sighs,
“ Behold in me, the source of all the woes,
“ That paled on thy fair cheek the early rose !
“ But thou art generous, and wilt kindly shed
“ Forgiveness on Ernesto’s aged head ;
“ Yes, thou wilt much allow to sad extremes,
“ For round thee, as a Light, Compassion beams !”

With pleas’d surprize my beating heart expands ;
My swifter tears fall copious on his hands ;

My

My trembling knee involuntary bends,
For deepeſt reverence with my tranſport blends.

' O Heaven! art thou that Being, ſo rever'd,
' In happier days to my charm'd Soul endear'd?
' Which oft, unconſcious of thy Form, ſurvey'd
' Thy worth, by filial tenderneſs diſplay'd.
' All, all is known!—no ſelfiſh murmurs riſe,
' Nor groans arraign the mandate of the ſkies;
' Nobly Eugenio their high call obey'd!—
' Oh! what a Wretch were I, ſhould I upbraid,
' Becauſe th' exalted Youth, whoſe heart I won,
' Deſerves the bleſſing, to be born thy Son!
' Some vagrant drops may fall, ſome rebel ſighs,
' Perchance, to our divided Loves ariſe;
' But vaniſh'd now is Miſery's ruthleſs ſmart,
' Tho' ſad, not wretched, my devoted Heart;
' And oh! ſince poor Louisa thus obtains
' Thy generous love, thy ſoothing pity gains,
' On them each fond regret ſhall ſink to reſt,
' Nor Memory whiſper, how ſhe once was bleſt.'

L   " Honor'd

" Honor'd LOUISA! fair angelic Maid,
" With every blessing be thy worth repaid !˙
" But Time flies rapidly !—the least delay
" Ill suits th' important message I convey ;
" An hapless Penitent adjures thee fly,
" To pardon, and receive her dying sigh ;
" O come with me, LOUISA !—at thy gates,
" Lo ! in the Glen, th' expecting chariot waits !"

Silent—astonish'd—trembling—faint—and pale,
My hurried step he hasten'd to the Vale ;
And soon, as seated by his side I rode,
Thus, from his lip, EMIRA's story flow'd.

' When to the Altar my unhappy Son
' Led the gay Bride, whom all unsought he won,
' Pensive his eye, and serious was his air ;
' Tho', with attentive, and respectful care,
' He strove to hide the sorrows of his Soul,
' But could not oft their bursting sigh controul,
' Bright, and adorn'd, as came the high-born Maid,
' In every lavish elegance array'd.

' Yet

'Yet oft I saw, that inauspicious Morn,
'From smother'd consciousness, the transient scorn
'Cast lurid flame at times, amid the joy
'That glow'd voluptuous in her ardent eye,
'When she perceiv'd, no ray of fond desire
'Met her warm glance, or authoris'd its fire;
'Saw deep-felt anguish in her Bridegroom prove
'The power supreme of violated Love;
'And oft his notice, courteous, yet constrain'd,
'Eager she sought; receiving it, disdain'd;
'And still each day increas'd the vain chagrin,
'And waked new sallies of malicious spleen;
'The pensive homage of a wounded Mind,
'Tho' grateful, sad, and, without ardor, kind,
'Seem'd to reproach those eyes, as powerless grown,
'Whose glance, she deem'd, might make the World her own.

'Unjust EMIRA! that could'st hope to gain
'Love's glowing homage from an Heart in pain;
'Thou should'st have sooth'd th' involuntary smart,
'And with his friendship satisfied thy heart;

'Thus

' Thus fweet, and gentle, thou had'ft quickly won
' That grateful tribute from my generous Son ;
' But well he knew, thy vain ill-govern'd Mind,
' Nor foft compaffion knew, nor love refined ;
' So unregretful faw thy wafted hours
' Refign'd to Diffipation's reftlefs powers ;
' Yet wifh'd thofe powers a kind relief might prove
' To the pain'd fenfe of difappointed Love ;
' And fometimes hoped, the ftrong maternal claims
' Might lead her light defires to fofter aims,
' When a fweet Cherub-Daughter bleft her arms,
' Whofe features promis'd all her Mother's charms ;
' But no maternal tendernefs fhe fhares,
' The gay EMIRA fcorns its gentle cares.

  ' And when to Pleafures, frivolous and vain,
' He faw fucceed, a mad licentious train ;
' Play, ruinoufly high, and dark Intrigue
' Prompt the wild wifh, and form the baneful league,
' How oft has he adjur'd her to reflect,
' What pricelefs peace her wild purfuits neglect !

                                        ' On

‘ On me propitious Heaven the power beftow’d

‘ To cancel the vaft debt my fortunes ow’d

‘ To proud EMIRA,—for my lucky Sails

‘ Return’d, rich freighted, from Hifpania’s vales;

‘ Thofe Sails, whofe venture rafh, and long delay,

‘ With all a Bankrupt’s mifery crofs’d my way.

‘ Now many a fmiling Chance combined to raife,

‘ Above the level of my faireft days,

‘ That Wealth, whofe dreadful and impending fall

‘ In one wide ruin had involv’d us all,

‘ But that EMIRA, in that fateful hour,

‘ Snatch’d my devoted credit from its power;

‘ And duteous, noble, dear EUGENIO ftood,

‘ A youthful Victim to his Father’s good.

‘ Yet when I faw, that mean unfeeling Pride

‘ Rul’d the vain bofom of the worthlefs Bride,

‘ My Soul rejoic’d, with intereft to repay

‘ The heavy debt of that difaftrous day;

‘ For what idea can more painful rife,

‘ Than much to owe, where owing we defpife?

‘ One

‘ One scene, alas ! my heart can ne'er forget,

‘ Nor Memory paint it without keen regret

‘ That in the female breaft, fo form'd to prove

‘ The fweet refinements of maternal Love,

‘ Difdain, and guilty Pleafure, fhould controul,

‘ And to its yearnings indurate the Soul.

‘ Confummate from her toilette's anxious tafk,

‘ E MIRA, haftening to the midnight Mafk,

‘ Th' Apartment enter'd, where EUGENIO ftood,

‘ And near me lean'd, in deeply mufing mood.

‘ My folding arms their rofy Infant preft

‘ To the fond throbbings of a Grandfire's breaft.

‘ She, with the tones of petulant reproach,

‘ And neck averted, call'd her tardy coach.

‘ I mark'd EUGENIO's difapproving figh,

‘ As the licentious veftment caught his eye ;

‘ The lofty turban, from whofe furface rais'd,

‘ Glitter'd the filver plume, the diamond blaz'd ;

‘ The fnowy veil, in foft diforder thrown,

‘ The bofom, rifing from the loofen'd zone,

‘ And

' And limbs, by golden muflin ill conceal'd,
' Whofe clinging folds their perfect form reveal'd.

  ' With heart-felt pain the injur'd Hufband faw
' The Fair thus fcorn Decorum's guardian law ;
' Saw all that decent drefs, that modeft pride,
' " Which doubles ev'ry charm it feeks to hide,"
' Once the bright Dame of Britain's lovelieft boaft,
' In the Seraglio's wanton Inmate loft !

  ' Seizing her ftruggling hand Eugenio tries
' To warn the fair Devoted, e'er fhe flies,
' Where Infamy in filent ambufh ftrays
' Amidft the antic Throng, the midnight blaze.

  " Oh ! is it thus, he faid, a wedded Dame
" Lights the loofe Profligate's difgraceful flame ?
" If 'gainft an Hufband's claim thy heart is fear'd,
" By Heaven eftablifh'd, and by Man revered,
" To that, if thy high Spirit fcorns to bend,
" Yet, O Emira ! hear me as thy Friend !

                           " Snatch

" Snatch thy bright youth, and all its countless charms,

" From a dread ambush of o'er-whelming harms,

" Whose Demon-tribe, some evils shall impart,

" To reach and wring the most obdurate heart !

" How will that haughty, that aspiring Mind,

" Which claims th' incessant homage of Mankind ;

" Sees to those Graces, flattering Crouds avow,

" Proud Rank unbend, and rival Beauty bow ;

" How will it bear to change this soft respect,

" For studied insolence, and rude neglect ?

" The nod familiar of the Coxcomb Throng ?

" Thy name the theme of their lascivious song ;

" And from the high-bred Dames, that now excite,

" And share the revels of thy dangerous night,

" Who, when Detection's livid spots arise,

" Will studious shun, affecting to despise ;

" Canst thou th' unbending knee's cold insult bear,

" Their smile of malice, and their vacant stare ?

" Shafts, which wrong'd Virtue only can sustain,

" And rise superior to th' unjust disdain."

' Thus

' Thus while he pour'd, to check this rash career,
' The startling questions on her wounded ear,
' Frowning she strove to disengage her hand,
' And fly the just reproach, the firm demand ;
' While sullen brows, and flashes of disdain,
' Too plainly prov'd the awful challenge vain.

' Then striving, from a softer cause, to impart
' The virtuous wish to her misguided heart,
' A Father's fondness melting in his look,
' From my embrace the smiling Babe he took ;
' Exclaiming, as in all its touching charms
' He gave it to her half-unwilling arms ;'

" Alas ! Emira, shall this Infant live
" To feel the grief that consciousness must give,
" When a dishonour'd Mother's deep disgrace
" Pours the pain'd crimson o'er the youthful face ?
" Or, lost to Virtue, thy example plead
" For the light manners, the licentious deed ?
" Forbid it Heaven !—O smile my Child, and lure,
" To the maternal transports, soft, and pure,

M   " That

" That lovely bofom!—let thy opening bloom
" Charm my EMIRA, e'er fhe yet confume,
" In guilty Pleafure's falfe and baneful flames,
" A Wife's fair faith—a Mother's tender claims!
" Oh! may fhe bid thee live to breathe her name
" Without the paufe of fear, the blufh of fhame!"

' She figh'd, and clafp'd the Infant to her breaft,
' And milder looks the yielding Heart confefs'd;
' Then, as its eyes to her's are rais'd the while
' With all the pathos of th' unconfcious fmile,
' Two cryftal drops, that Nature's influence fpeak,
' Steal from her lids, and wander down her cheek;
' Thofe ftranger tears, by that fweet thrill beguil'd,
' Fall on the forehead of her beauteous Child.
' Pleas'd the maternal tribute to furvey,
' EUGENIO kifs'd the lucid drops away.
' Earneft on him the Fair-One's moiften'd eyes
' Turn!—and fome rays benign of foft furprife
' Meet his kind gaze—but ah! the tranfient dawn
' Of virtuous feeling, inftant is withdrawn;

' And

' And thofe mild beams, that Beauty beft adorn,
' Sink in the clouds of recollected Scorn.

' Her arms extending, with imperious air,
' The fmiling Babe again to my fond care
' Coldly fhe gives ;—and giving it exclaims,'
—" Go little Wretch !—of tender mutual flames
" Thou wert not born !—then why fhould I embrace,
" And live for thee, whofe birth is my difgrace ?"

' Now to her Hufband, with contemptuous fmiles,
' She bends—and thus his guardian-care reviles.'
—" Louisa's Lover has a right to claim
" The ftern protection of Emira's fame !
" Whofe wealth, whofe rank, whofe youth, and far-famed
" So madly given to thy infenfate arms,   [charms,
" Are weak to chace the defpicable pains,
" That load thy heart, and ice thy torpid veins ;
" E'en now my Soul that mean regret efpies
" Pale on thy cheek, and languid in thine eyes !

M 2   " For

" For me, thy needlefs apprehenfion fpare!

" My peace, my fame, abjure EUGENIO's care!

" And in my bofom female Pride fhall prove

" An happier guard, than my weak, wafted love!

" Farewell Infenfible!—enjoy thy grief!

" Seek in inglorious fhades, and fighs, relief

" For the *hard* doom relentlefs Fate ordain'd,

" Thy *fplendid* fortunes to *EMIRA's* chain'd!—

" She goes to join, too great of Soul to mourn,

" The Circles fhe was deftin'd to adorn,

" Till, feizing on her heart with demon-hold,

" Paffion *infane* that Deftiny controul'd!"

' And thus the Fair, that one fhort minute faw

' Obey the facred force of Nature's law;

' Now to its dictates more obdurate grown,

' To Danger's paths with double zeft is flown.

' Then to the famenefs of the Opera Throng,

' Where vocal tricks fuftain th' infipid fong;

' Where, round the Dancer, echoing plaudits found,

' At each indecent and diftorted bound,

' Each

‘ Each odious gefture that ufurps the place
‘ Of eafy Elegance and genuine Grace;
‘ To the pain'd hope, the fecret dread prefage,
‘ Th' ignoble triumph, and the fmother'd rage
‘ Of fatal Play;—the Ball's fatiguing tafk,
‘ And the loofe revel of the wanton mafk;
‘ To thefe fucceed, th' appointed guilty hour,
‘ That vefts the Libertine with boundlefs power;
‘ Whofe darling hope confifts not in the joy
‘ He fcarce has wifh'd, and that fhall inftant cloy,
‘ But in the triumph his mean pride has won,
‘ When, public as the Air, and Noon-day Sun,
‘ The dup'd unhappy Fair-One's crimes fhall throw
‘ New fancied glories round the Boafter's brow.

‘ Behold EMIRA, loft to faith, and fhame,
‘ Quench the laft fpark of her long faded fame
‘ For him, whofe gay attentions to fecure,
‘ Rafh Beauty fpreads the felf-enfnaring lure;
‘ That haughty Lord, licentious, falfe, and vain,
‘ Whofe groveling heart, nor rank, nor charms obtain;
                                        ‘ A fwarthy

‘ A fwarthy Opera Dancer triumphs there,

‘ And foils th’ attractions of the high-born Fair ;

‘ For her he wears the abject, lafting chains ;

‘ To her, of Fafhion’s drudgery complains,

‘ When in feign’d tranfports veiling cold diftafte,

‘ With dames of Quality his moments wafte ;

‘ Wafte, to fupport his confequence, and prove

‘ His fway refiftlefs in the realms of Love ;

‘ While by her venal arts himfelf enflaved,

‘ Poor from her fquandering, by her humors braved,

‘ He hugs the Bonds, round which, to grace their power,

‘ Nor Youth, nor Beauty twine one blooming flower.

‘ On him EMIRA her unvalued charms,

‘ Scarce afk’d, beftows, to wake the wifh’d alarms

‘ Of Sifter-Beauties, and enjoy their pain,

‘ Their dangerous fpleen, and rivalry infane.

‘ Too well the haughty Dames avenge the fmart

‘ Her fhort-liv’d triumph coft their fwelling heart,

‘ As her falfe Lover, with abandon’d pride,

‘ Reveals the guilt, which Honor bids him hide !

‘ Nor

‘ Nor tamely had an injur’d Hufband borne
‘ Of her connubial faith this lavifh fcorn,
‘ But that his own remembered coldnefs brought
‘ Some palliation to his generous thought
‘ For guilty Beauty, in thefe fenfual times,
‘ Where foreign fafhions lead to foreign crimes;
‘ Then, that her wealth, when Fortune’s ftorm arofe,
‘ Saved his loved Parents from impending woes!
‘ Oh! ’twas a thought that would no mark allow
‘ Of juft refentment for her broken vow,
‘ Save, that he leaves the violated bed,
‘ Where Peace no gentle poppy e’er had fhed,
‘ And ftudioufly each day avoids the Dame,
‘ Who ftains his honor with her bleeding fame.

‘ By Duty urged, by Friendfhip warned in vain,
‘ As gay EMIRA drives with loofened rein,
‘ Proud Diffipation’s wearying labyrinths prove
‘ The bane of Health, as the difgrace of Love.
‘ ’Midft the light Throngs, that croud the garifh Mart,
‘ Confuming Fever hurls her fiery dart;

‘ Deep

' Deep in E M I R A's breaſt behold it ſtand,

' And Life's warm current ſhrink beneath the Brand !

 ' 'Tis now ſhe wakens to the painful ſenſe

' Of deep contrition for her paſt offence ;

' And now, alas ! her dying eyes ſurvey

' The Form of guilty Pleaſure paſs away ;

' Drop the gay maſk, and throw the ghaſtly ſmile

' Back on the baffled Victim of her guile.

 ' Hapleſs E M I R A on her dying bed

' Shrinks from the Phantom with convulſive dread ;

' While Conſcience rous'd, her former guilt recalls,

' And with E U G E N I O's wrongs her heart appals.

' Unfelt till this ſad hour, the ſtrong controul

' Of genuine fondneſs ruſhes on her Soul !

' But with her native violence it reigns,

' Aids the Diſeaſe, and ſtimulates its pains.

' Her Huſband's name, in tones of ſtrange affright,

' Eager ſhe breathes, nor bears him from her ſight.

' In vain her calmneſs gently he intreats,

' The generous pardon vainly he repeats ;

' For,

' For, ftarting from her couch, fhe ftill demands
' Pardon afrefh, and wildly wrings his hands.
' You too, LOUISA, fhe invokes, to fign
' Her paffport bleft to Mercy's healing fhrine.'
" O dear ERNESTO," the fhrill accents cry,
" If you have pity, to LOUISA fly;
" Sweet, injur'd Excellence! would fhe impart
" Her pardon to this felf-accufing Heart,
" 'Twould cheer my Spirit, hov'ring on its flight
" To the dark confines of ETERNAL NIGHT."

' She faid—and dear LOUISA will beftow
' Th' adjur'd forgivenefs on repentant woe;
' Will feel its fufferings all her wrongs atone,
' And in EMIRA's pangs forget her own.'

ERNESTO ceas'd—for Pity's throbs opprefs'd
With tender force his venerable breaft.
Thro' the remaining way our mutual fighs,
From awe-ftruck thought, in folemn filence rife.

Shuddering

Shuddering we now draw near the houfe of Death,
And find yet ftays the intermitting breath.
What agitated dread my bofom tears,
When paufing we afcend the filent ftairs!—
As we approach the flowly opening door!—
As my pain'd Senfes, horror-chill'd, explore
The dim Apartment, where the leffen'd light
Gives the pale Sufferer to my fearful fight!
The matchlefs grace of that confummate Frame
Withering beneath the Fever's fcorching flame.
Outftretch'd and wan, with laboring breath fhe lies,
Clofing in palfied lids her quivering eyes.
EUGENIO's hand lock'd in her clafping hands,
As hufh'd and mournful by her couch he ftands!—
Horror, and Pity mingled traces flung,
Which o'er his Form, like wintry fhadows, hung;
Yet, on my entrance in that dreary Room,
A gleam of Joy darts thro' their awful gloom!
Oh! what a moment!—my EUGENIO's face!—
Alas!—how faded its once glowing grace!
Paft hours of woe on his pale cheek I read,
In eyes whofe beams, like waining ftars, recede!

Faintly

Faintly the found of that known voice I hear,
" Oh my LOUISA!" fcarce it meets my ear,
Left the imperfect flumber fhould be found
Chas'd by the check'd involuntary found.
But clear the fenfes of the Dying feem,
Like the expiring taper's flafhing beam.
Scarce audibly tho' breath'd, LOUISA's name
EMIRA hears, and her enfeebled Frame,
With fudden powerlefs effort, ftrives to raife;
But, finking back, her eyes, in eager gaze,
Are fix'd on mine,—what anguifh in their beams!
O confcious Guilt! how dreadful thy extremes!
The chill numb hands, whence deadly dews had broke,
Snatch'd from her Lord's, when ftarting fhe awoke,
Now, as they feem unable to extend,
Softly I take, as o'er her couch I bend;
She turns away, oppreft by thought'fevere,
And fteeps her pillow in the bitter tear.

Alas! be calm! be comforted! I cried,
" Do you too pardon?"—fhrilly fhe replied,

Bending

Bending again on me that burning ray,

Whofe heat no contrite waters could allay.

" Then, dear Louisa, peaceful fhall I die,

" Since hallow'd thus my laft—remorfeful figh ;

" But Oh ! 'tis dread—when Memory difplays

" The guilt-ftain'd retrofpect of vanifh'd days !

" The fecret—felfifh joy—which hail'd the blow,

" That laid Ernesto's profperous fortunes low ;

" Sever'd thofe hands—whofe glowing hearts were join'd,

" The facred union of the kindred Mind.——

" Heaven reunites them !—and the Wretch removes,

" That impious rofe between their plighted Loves ;

" Who not content to blaft their fweet increafe,

" And arm—Eugenio's Virtue—'gainft his Peace,

" Added"——But now, from feeblenefs, or fhame,

A deadly faintnefs fickens thro' her Frame.

Reviving fhortly— " I would fain," fhe cries,

" E'er everlafting darknefs clofe thefe eyes,

" Intreat of that kind Spirit—fweet, and mild,

" Its future—generous goodnefs—to my Child.

" Love her, Louisa—love her—I implore,

" When loft Emira—wounds thy peace no more !

" Oh !

" Oh! gently foster in her opening Youth,

" The feeds of Virtue—Honor—Faith—and Truth,

" For thy Eugenio's fake!—who gave her birth,

" And gave—I trust—the temper of his worth!

" And when—on his lov'd knees—my Infant climbs,

" Adjure him—to forget her Mother's crimes!

" I know thou wilt!—I feel thy heart expand,

" In the dear preffure—of that gentle hand.

" O ye wrong'd pair! in the laft awful Morn,

" When my ftain'd Soul at the eternal Bourn

" Shall trembling ftand—her final doom to hear,

" She lefs fhall dread—to meet the injur'd there!

" Congenial Mercy—fhe may hope to prove,

" From the offended Powers—of Truth—and Love!"

While yet thefe interrupted accents hung,

Faint on the rigid lip, and faltering tongue,

The ftiffening fpafm, the fuffocating breath,

Gave dread prefage of near approaching Death.—

Now roll the eyes in fierce and reftlefs gaze!

Now on their wildnefs fteals the ghaftly glaze!

Till

Till o'er her Form the fhadowy horrors fpread
The dim fuffufion that involves the DEAD.

Thus Wealth, and Rank, and all their gorgeous Train,
The Proud that madden, and enfnare the Vain ;
Youth's frolic grace, and Beauty's radiant bloom,
Sink, in the dreary filence of the Tomb ;
But oh ! rejoice with me, that Hope's bleft beam
Threw o'er the dark Abyfs one trembling gleam !

For thy LOUISA—Words can ill impart
How dear the comforts eddying round her heart !
How foft the Joy, by Sorrow's fhading hand
Touch'd into charms more exquifitely bland !
Or paint EUGENIO's tranfports as they rife,
More fweet for generous Pity's mingled fighs ;
Sweet above all, from the exulting pride
Of felf-approving Virtue, ftrongly tried.
Applauding CONSCIENCE, yes ! to thee 'tis given,
To infpire a Joy, that antedates our Heaven !

Thus,

Thus, on Moriah's confecrated height,
Flow'd the obedient Patriarch's fond delight,
When o'er the filial breaft, his faith to feal,
On high had gleam'd the facrificing Steel;
Thus flow'd, when at the Voice, divinely mild,
His raptured hands unbound his only Child!

O come, my EMMA!—yet thou ne'er haft feen
Embodied Virtue in EUGENIO's Mein;
Grace, grandeur, truth, and tendernefs combin'd,
The liberal effluence of the polifh'd Mind!
And for more generous pleafures than we prove,
The blifs furveying of the Friends we love,
Sure we muft wait, till Angels fhall impart
Their own perfection to th' expanded Heart!

Hafte then to fhare our bleffings, as they glow
Thro' the receding fhades of heavieft woe!——
As Spring's fair Morn, with calm, and dewy light,
Breaks thro' the weary, long, and ftormy Night,
So now, as thro' the Vale of Life we ftray,
The STAR of JOY relumes, and leads us on our way!

F I N I S.